Lost and Found

Kids Can Read ® Kids Can Read is a registered trademark of Kids Can Press Ltd.

Kids Can Press acknowledges the financial support of the Government of Ontario,
through the Ontario Media Development Corporation's Ontario Book Initiative; the
Ontario Arts Council; the Canada Council for the Arts; and the Government of Canada,
through the BPIDP, for our publishing activity.

Published in Canada by
Kids Can Press Ltd.
29 Birch Avenue
Toronto, ON M4V 1E2

Published in the U.S. by
Kids Can Press Ltd.
2250 Military Road
Tonawanda, NY 14150

www.kidscanpress.com

Adapted by David MacDonald and Adrienne Mason from the book *The Carnival Caper*.

Edited by David MacDonald
Designed by Kathleen Gray

Printed and bound in Singapore

The hardcover edition of this book is smyth sewn casebound.
The paperback edition of this book is limp sewn with a drawn-on cover.

CM 07 0 9 8 7 6 5 4 3 2 1
CM PA 07 0 9 8 7 6 5 4 3 2 1

Library and Archives Canada Cataloguing in Publication

Mason, Adrienne
    Lost and found / written by Adrienne Mason ; illustrated by PatCupples. —Rev. ed.

(Kids Can read)
Previously published under title: Sound off.

ISBN 978-1-55453-251-3 (bound).--ISBN 978-1-55453-252-0 (pbk.)

1. Sound—Juvenile fiction. 2. Dogs—Juvenile fiction. 3. Sound—
Juvenile literature. I. Cupples, Patricia II. Title. III. Title: Mason,
Adrienne. Sound off. IV. Series: Kids Can read (Toronto, Ont.)

QC225.5.M38 2008   jC813'.54   C2007-902845-4

Kids Can Press is a ℓ☺ⁿUS™ Entertainment company

Lost and Found

Written by Adrienne Mason

Illustrated by Pat Cupples

Kids Can Press

Lu and Clancy were best friends.

They were dog detectives, too.

They found lost mittens,

and stolen kites,

and missing kittens,

and sometimes more.

But now, they were babysitting

two puppies.

They were taking care

of Lu's sister.

Her name was Sophie.

They were also babysitting

Sophie's friend, Fanny.

"Time for your nap," Clancy told

Sophie and Fanny.

"I want a snack!" said Fanny.

"I want a story!" said Sophie.

Then Fanny threw a water balloon.

"They do not seem very sleepy,"

said Clancy.

"We need to tire those pups out,"

said Lu.

"Let's go on a hike to Magic Lake!"

said Clancy.

Lu put a few things into her backpack.

"I am ready," she said.

"I am almost ready," said Clancy.

He had a huge pile of stuff.

"Why do you need all that?"

asked Lu.

"You never know," said Clancy.

"You might get caught

in the snow."

"Or see a pretty bird."

"Or need to solve a crime."

"I am ready for anything!" he said.

Clancy filled up his backpack.

Then he tied more things to the outside.

"You cannot carry all that!" said Lu.

"Oh, yes I can," said Clancy.

He struggled and stumbled,

and finally he stood up.

"We are off to Magic Lake!"

Everyone walked and walked.

Soon Sophie sat down.

"I am hot," she said.

"I am thirsty," said Fanny.

"Wait for me!" Clancy called from behind.

"Maybe this was not a good idea after all,"

thought Lu.

The four friends kept on walking.

They stopped to take a nap.

They stopped while Clancy

searched through his backpack.

Then they stopped to have a snack.

Sophie and Fanny did not want

to rest any more.

They wanted to swim.

"Let's go!" said Sophie.

Finally, they reached Magic Lake.

"We are here!" said Sophie and Fanny.

Everyone was ready for a swim.

"Look out below!" shouted Clancy.

Kersploosh!

He did a belly flop into the lake.

Then Lu spotted a big, black cloud.

"Storm coming! Take cover!" she cried.

The pups dashed into the bushes.

Suddenly, there was a yell.

Then there was a scream.

"Sophie!" cried Lu.

"Where are you?"

Lu and Clancy ran into the bushes.

Sophie was gone!

All they found was her bathing suit.

It was time for dog detectives

Lu and Clancy to get to work.

Clancy grabbed his camera

to snap pictures of clues.

"It is starting to rain!" said Lu.

"Run for that cave."

Thunder crashed and lightning flashed.

The wind blew,

and the rain kept pouring down.

Puddles became ponds.

"Sophie!" called Lu.

"Sophie!" called Clancy.

There was no answer.

Where could Sophie be?

"I am going to look for Sophie,"

said Clancy.

He ran to his backpack

and pulled out a raincoat.

Then he pulled out an umbrella.

"I just knew these would

come in handy," he said.

Then Lu and Fanny heard

a very scary sound.

"Clancy, did you hear that?"

called Lu.

Clancy ran back to the cave.

"It sounded like a moose —

a very angry moose!" he said.

"I am scared," cried Fanny.

"I am going to look around," said Lu.

She stepped out of the cave.

The scary sound started again.

It seemed to be coming from a bush.

Lu jumped back into the cave.

The sound stopped.

"I wonder ..." said Lu.

"Clancy, did you bring a fishing net?"

asked Lu.

"I sure did," said Clancy.

Lu got the net from the backpack.

Lu and Clancy crept toward the bush.

"Be careful!" called Fanny.

They heard the scary sound once more.

Then they heard a giggle.

Quick as a flash, Lu snapped down the net.

"Gotcha!" she cried.

It was Sophie inside the net!

Lu and Clancy did not have time to be mad.

It was getting late.

They pulled Sophie from the net

and ran back to the cave.

"Time to head home," said Lu.

"Which way is home?" asked Fanny.

"This way," pointed Clancy.

"No, this way," pointed Lu.

It was raining.

It was getting dark.

And now they were lost!

"I am cold," said Fanny.

"I am hungry," said Sophie.

"What are we going to do?"

"We will have to stay here for the night,"

said Lu.

"Stay here in the cave?" asked Sophie.

"All night?" asked Fanny.

They looked scared.

"Do not worry," said Clancy.

"I brought everything we need."

Clancy grabbed his backpack.

He pulled out blankets, a lantern,

playing cards and a can of soup.

And that was not all.

Soon Clancy had made the cave

as warm and cozy as home.

The pups settled in for the night.

Lu woke up and rubbed her eyes.

The storm was over.

All she heard was snoring dogs.

"Wake up," she said.

"We need to make noise

so someone can find us."

"How about this noise?" said Clancy.

He rolled over and snored some more.

"Then I will have to make noise myself,"

said Lu.

She screamed.

She yelled.

She whistled.

But no one came to rescue them.

"What are we going to do now?"

asked Sophie.

"We need to make noisier noise," said Lu.

She pulled some things

out of Clancy's backpack.

Lu made a drum for Sophie

and a flute for Fanny.

The pups made LOTS of noise.

Soon, someone did come to rescue them.

Before long, the pups were home again.

But they still made lots of noise!

Lu and Clancy did not mind.

They just smiled

and put on

their earmuffs.

Toot on a Flute!

You can make a flute just
like the one Lu made for Fanny.

Here is what you will need:

- 2 large drinking straws
- scissors
- sticky tape

1. Cut the straws into four pieces.
Make each piece a
different length.

2. Lay the straws on a table.
Line up the straws at one end.
Then tape them together.

3. Blow across the tops of the straws to
make sounds.